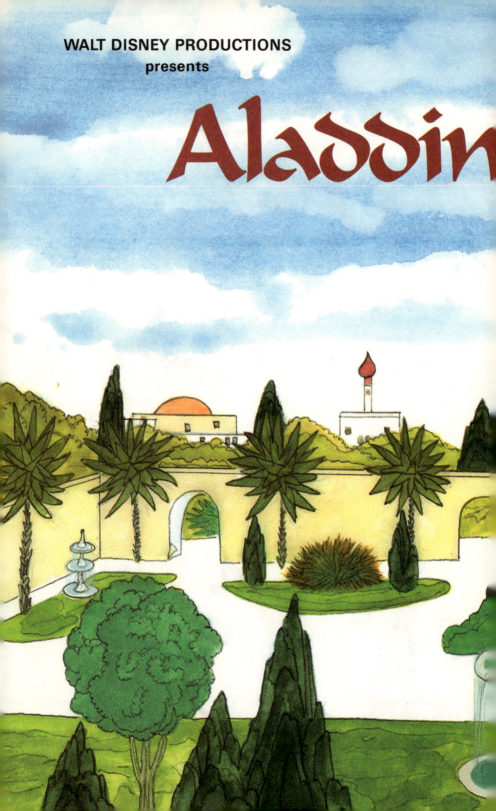

WALT DISNEY PRODUCTIONS
presents

Aladdin

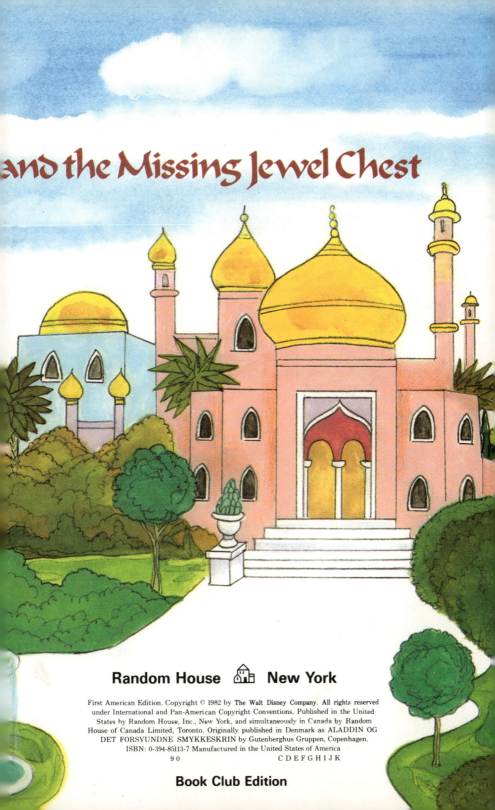

and the Missing Jewel Chest

Random House 🏠 **New York**

First American Edition. Copyright © 1982 by The Walt Disney Company. All rights reserved under International and Pan-American Copyright Conventions. Published in the United States by Random House, Inc., New York, and simultaneously in Canada by Random House of Canada Limited, Toronto. Originally published in Denmark as ALADDIN OG DET FORSVUNDNE SMYKKESKRIN by Gutenberghus Gruppen, Copenhagen. ISBN: 0-394-85113-7 Manufactured in the United States of America
9 0   C D E F G H I J K

Book Club Edition

Princess Minnie and her husband
Aladdin, lived in the royal palace.

But now Aladdin was away
on a trip.

And Minnie's father, the sultan,
was at his new summer palace
by the seashore.

So Minnie carefully guarded
Aladdin's magic lamp.

Minnie heard hoofbeats
in the courtyard.
Aladdin was returning
from his trip.

"Oh, Aladdin, you are just
in time!" called Minnie.
"We have to make some plans!"

A new guard stood at the door.
"Hmm, where have I seen that
face before?" wondered Aladdin.
He did not guess that the guard was
a wicked magician in disguise.
This magician had wanted Aladdin's
magic lamp for a long time.

"It is good to
be home," said
Aladdin. "Now,
what should we
make plans for?"

"My father's birthday is very soon,"
said Minnie. "But he is so far away.
How can we have a party for him?"

Just then,
a messenger
arrived with
a letter.

The princess opened
the letter.
"It is from my
father!" Minnie said.

Dear Minnie and Aladdin,
    Please come visit my new palace at the seashore. I am going to have a big birthday party.

    Love,

    Father

"It is a long way to the seashore,"
said Aladdin. "We must leave as soon
as we can."

Minnie and
Aladdin hurried
off to pack.

Minnie picked out dozens of
her prettiest dresses.
    And she decided to take
her whole chest of jewels.

Aladdin picked
out his favorite
turbans.

It was hard to
choose!

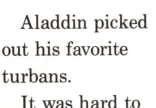

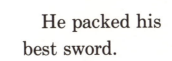

He packed his
best sword.

"And I must take
my magic medal,"
said Aladdin.

If Aladdin rubbed
the medal, a genie
would appear.

Then Aladdin remembered his magic lamp.
"It is the most valuable thing I own,"
said Aladdin. "I must take it with me."
The lamp had made Aladdin rich.
And it had helped him to marry Minnie.

So Aladdin carefully packed the lamp
with Princess Minnie's jewels.

He did not see the new guard
watching him.

The next morning, the royal couple
was ready to leave.

Princess Minnie
climbed onto the royal
elephant.

She held the jewel
chest on her lap.

The new guard rode
behind Minnie to keep
her safe—or so she
thought.

But the evil guard
had plans of his own.

The royal party
moved out throug
the palace gate.

Aladdin was in the lead on
his strong white horse.
For days the group rode across
the wide lands of the sultan.

The royal party climbed steep
and dangerous mountains.

Aladdin stayed
bravely in the lead.
The guard sat
behind the princess.
He kept his eye on
the jewel chest.

One night, the magician was ready to act.

In the night, the magician took the
jewel chest with the magic lamp in it.
Then he stole a horse and rode away.
His home was in the nearby mountains.

The next morning,
Aladdin saw that
the jewel chest
was missing.

"The magic lamp i
gone, too!" Aladdin
groaned.

The new guard and a horse were gone.
Then Aladdin knew the truth.
The guard was really the magician
disguise!

Aladdin and the others searched for the magician all day.

Then Aladdin remembere his magic medal.

He rubbed it, and at onc a genie appeared.

Aladdin told the genie what had happened.

"I have no power over the lamp," said the genie. "But I can take you to it."

"Good!" said Aladdin. "Let's go!"

Soon Aladdin was flying away
on a magic carpet.

By nighttime, the magician was home.
He unpacked the magic lamp and smiled.
The lamp was his at last!

Then the evil magician went to bed.

Aladdin flew through the starry night
on his magic carpet.

The carpet slowed down when it reached
the magician's home.

Then the carpet glided
down to the rooftop
of the house.

Aladdin crept down the stairs
to the magician's bedroom.

Without a sound, Aladdin picked up
the lamp and put it in the jewel chest.

Quietly, Aladdin crept out of the room with the chest.

But just outside, he bumped into a large jar.

The jar fell over and broke.

CRASH!

The magician angrily awoke.

Aladdin raced for the stairs.

The magician ran after
Aladdin.

Aladdin reached the roo
just in time.

He jumped onto the magic carpet
nd flew away.
The jewels and the lamp were saved!

By dawn, Aladdin was
safely back in camp.

"My hero!" said Princess Minnie. "I am
so glad you are back! But now we have
lost a day. Tomorrow is my father's
birthday. How will we get there in time?"

"We will ride on my magic carpet,"
said Aladdin.

Away they flew over the countryside.
Hours later, they reached the beach.

"Look!" said Aladdin.

He pointed to a palace below them.

'That must be my father's summer home," said Minnie. "Let's land here."

The sultan was happy
to see Minnie and Aladdin.
"Welcome!" he shouted.
"How was your trip?"

"We had quite an adventure," Aladdin
said as they sat down to dinner.
When the sultan heard their tale,
he cheered.

At the sultan's birthday party the next day, Princess Minnie and Aladdin were the happiest couple there.

They had made it to the party in time.

And they had rescued the jewel chest with the magic lamp!